Milli, Jack and the Dancing Cat

words and pictures
Stephen Michael King

ALLEN&UNWIN

For: Enja   Tanith &   Joey &
             Luka   Danielle,
                         Peter & Anke
                         (water fountains for weary travelers)

A big Thank you to: Rosalind, Trish and Margaret C

First published in 2003
First paperback edition published in 2004

Allen & Unwin
83 Alexander St
Crows Nest NSW 2065
Australia
Phone: (61 2) 8425 0100
Fax: (61 2) 9906 2218
Email: info@allenandunwin.com
Web: www.allenandunwin.com

National Library of Australia
Cataloguing-in-Publication entry:

King, Stephen Michael
Milli, Jack and the dancing cat

ISBN 1 86508 748 3. - 10 9 8 7 6 5 4 3 2
ISBN 1 86508 747 5 (pbk.). - 10 9 8 7 6 5 4 3 2 1

1. Girls - Juvenile fiction. 2. Minstrels - Juvenile fiction.
3. Cats - Juvenile fiction. I. Title.

A823.3

Cover and text design by Stephen Michael King
Set in 22 pt Bronte by Stephen Michael King
Printed in Singapore by Imago Productions

Other books by
STEPHEN MICHAEL KING:

WORDS AND PICTURES:

The Man Who Loved Boxes
Patricia
Henry and Amy
Emily Loves to Bounce

PICTURES:

Beetle Soup
The Little Blue Parcel
Amelia Ellicott's Garden
Pocket Dogs
Where does Thursday Go?
Serena and the Sea Serpent
Goblin in the Bush

$\mathcal{M}$illi could take a thing
that was a nothing . . .

and make it . . .

a something!

She found things other people threw away . . .

forgotten things,

rusty things.

She cut them,

bent them,

pulled them apart

and joined them
together in amazing ways.

Milli could take a straight piece
of wire and give it a wiggle,
or a simple square of cloth
and set it sailing in the wind.

But the people in her town only wanted
ordinary, practical, familiar things.
They rushed here and bustled there
with no time for anything that was
a little different.

So, instead of doing
what she loved most,

Milli spent her days
making

brown shoes,

black shoes

and plain, ordinary
work boots.

Night after night Milli dreamed she was brave enough
to show everyone what she could really do.

But day after day was the same as before.

Then one morning, two vagabond minstrels
from faraway places trudged into town . . .

Jack and the Dancing Cat.

Jack could hear humming, and the sound of
someone's feet shuffling a rough old dance
on a dusty floor.

'It's coming from that shoe shop,' said Cat.

There was something odd about the place
that they liked.
'Let's go and see,' said Jack.
'Meeow,' said Cat.

So they waltzed right in.
'I'm Jack,' said Jack,
'I'm Cat,' said Cat.
'Oh! I'm . . . I'm Milli,'
said Milli, in surprise.
'It looks as though you two
need new boots!'
Cat showed her their
empty purse.

'Perhaps we could give you
dancing lessons, in exchange,'
said Jack, with a bow.
Milli smiled.

Jack and Cat taught Milli
all the dances they knew.

They did tap

and jazz

and ballet.

They did the two-step,
the three-step

and the tricky twisting
backward sliding four-step.

Sometimes they just wobbled,

fooled around and floated,

or pretended they had branches,
like a tree.

Dancing made Milli feel

brave and free.

Milli loved her new friends,
and all the odd things about them.
She wanted to surprise them with
more than just plain, ordinary boots.

So, she made instruments with sounds that had never been heard before,

and curly-toed shoes covered in stars, and purple satin slippers with bells.

There were clothes to match, patterned and painted by hand, and sewn with care.

And while Milli was making
things for Jack and Cat . . .

she also made things for herself . . .

a soft, swirling dress
especially for dancing,

a fantastic water fountain

and a wiggly wonderful seat
to sit outside her front door.

Jack and Cat still had faraway places to explore,
but they stayed a little longer to help Milli
make some changes.

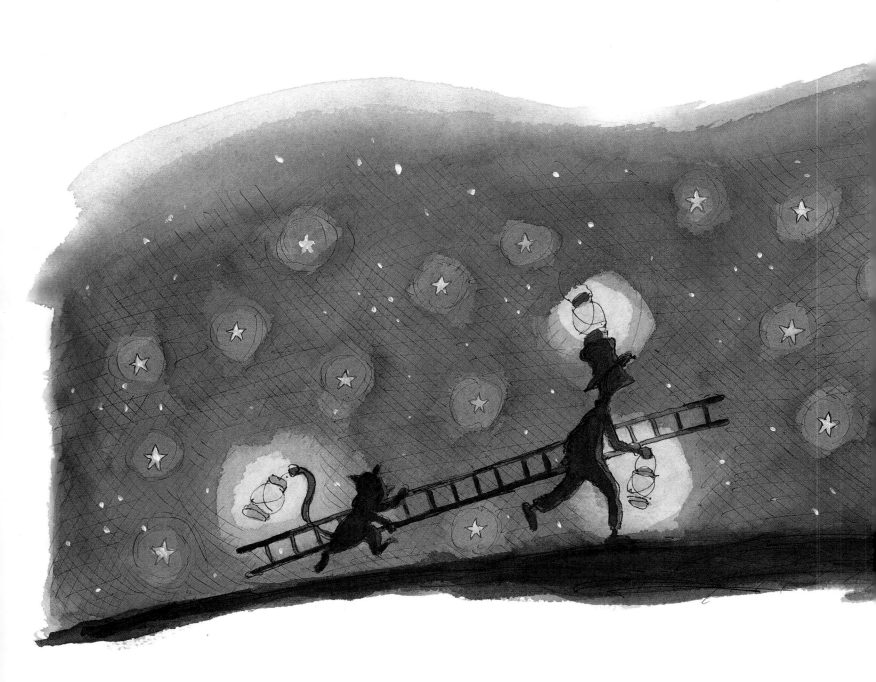

By the time Milli had done the finishing touches,
her shop was so spectacular that people came
from far and wide to see it.

Even the townspeople slowed down for a look.

And nothing, after that,
was ever the same as before.

Jack and Cat set off, taking all the extraordinary things Milli had made for them.

Everywhere they went, people stopped to watch them perform, and it wasn't long before 'Jack and the Dancing Cat' were renowned as the greatest wandering minstrels in all the land.

Milli never again

made a

plain,

ordinary

anything . . .